For Bella and Freddie – L.N.
For Viv and Davey – C.R.

ORCHARD BOOKS
First published in Great Britain in 2008 by Orchard Books
This edition first published in 2020 by The Watts Publishing Group

1 3 5 7 9 10 8 6 4 2

Text © Linda Newbery 2008
Illustrations © Catherine Rayner 2008

The moral rights of the author and illustrator have been asserted.
All rights reserved. A CIP catalogue record for this
book is available from the British Library.

ISBN 978 1 40836 089 7

Printed and bound in China

FSC
www.fsc.org

MIX
Paper from
responsible sources
FSC® C104740

Orchard Books
An imprint of Hachette Children's Group
Part of The Watts Publishing Group Limited
Carmelite House, 50 Victoria Embankment,
London EC4Y 0DZ

An Hachette UK Company
www.hachette.co.uk
www.hachettechildrens.co.uk

Posy

Linda Newbery

Catherine Rayner

ORCHARD

Posy!

She's a . . .

. . . whiskers wiper,

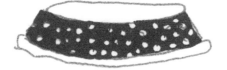

Crayon swiper.

Playful wrangler,

Knitting tangler.

Spider catcher,

Sofa scratcher.

Pillow
sitter,

Hissy
spitter!

Squabble
stirrer,

Charming
purrer.

Mirror
puzzler,

Ice cream
guzzler.

Sandwich
checker,

Board game
wrecker!

Leaf
collector,

Sock
inspector.

Tomcat fearer,

DISAPPEARER!

Dusk returner,

Cuddle earner!

Cushion clawer,

Sprawly snorer.

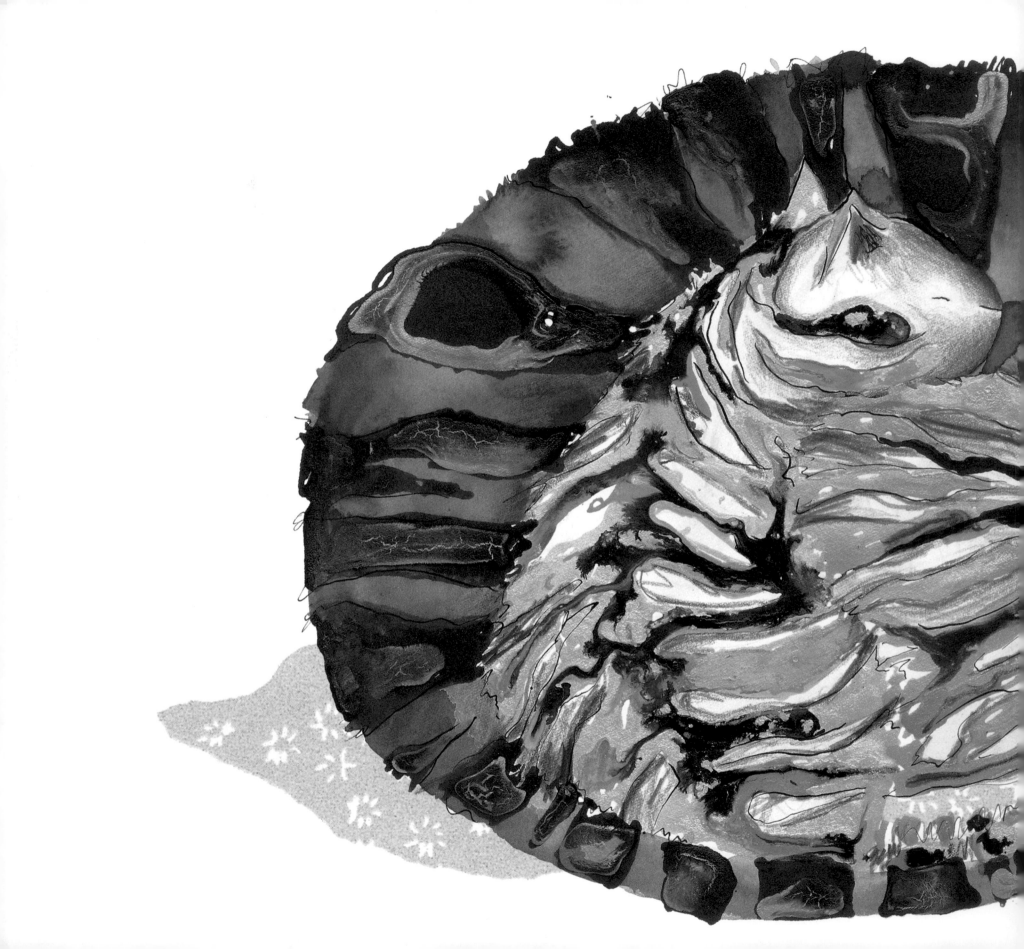

Posy!